Stranger to the Moon

T0022844

Evelio Rosero

Stranger to the Moon
a novel

*translated
by Victor Meadowcroft
& Anne McLean*

A NEW DIRECTIONS PAPERBOOK ORIGINAL

Manufactured in the United States of America
First published as a New Directions Book in 2021
Design by Erik Rieselbach

Library of Congress Cataloging-in-Publication Data
Names: Rosero Diago, Evelio, 1958– author. | Meadowcroft, Victor, translator. |
McLean, Anne, 1962– translator.
Title: Stranger to the moon : a novel / Evelio Rosero ;
translated by Victor Meadowcroft and Anne McLean.
Other titles: Señor que no conoce la luna. English
Description: New York : New Directions Publishing, 2021.
Identifiers: LCCN 2021021189 | ISBN 9780811228626 (paperback ; acid-free paper)
| ISBN 9780811228626 (ebook)
Subjects: LCGFT: Novels.
Classification: LCC PQ8180.28.O7 S4613 2021 | DDC 863/.64—dc23
LC record available at https://lccn.loc.gov/2021021189

10 9 8 7 6 5 4 3 2 1

New Directions Books are published for James Laughlin
by New Directions Publishing Corporation
80 Eighth Avenue, New York 10011

Stranger to the Moon

IT'S TRUE THAT THIS HOUSE IS ENORMOUS, BUT THERE are just too many of us. In order for us all to live here, there must always be one, at least, inside the wardrobe.

And it's usually me who lives in the wardrobe.

I could claim this wardrobe is my home. It's a relatively uncomfortable dwelling smelling of mold; but it's not without its advantages, because over time, my nails have managed to bore a little hole that serves as a window, so I can watch everything happening outside, without anybody knowing what's happening with me in here.

There are even times when they forget about me, and I have to poke my head out and yell so they remember I exist. I yell, and they might bring me a bowl of soup, if I'm lucky. I yell, and they might say I can come out. When this happens, I must first wait for someone to leave the house; then, I hear a dull thud on my door and the question:

"Still alive in there?"

"Still here," I say.

"You can come out now," they tell me. "Someone's gone outside."

I open the door, and come out. I don't come out, I emerge, I slide, I'm a long, rickety vapor; there's mist in my armpits, and my mouth is white, I'm a spatula of gelatin, I awaken to pain, splutter moans, I'm a roar, my foamy body fizzes with pins and needles, my eyes are stung red by the light, my eyes, desperate to make out the world, spin amid the hot fumes of the torches. On top of this, I have to wrestle my way through the multitude of naked yellow bodies that wander, compact and clammy, across the concrete court-yards and the tortuous, brightly lit corridors. But I make an effort and manage to adapt quickly; otherwise this body—as if it were another wardrobe confining me, helpless to begin with—could end up shattered, crushed, disappeared.

I don't bother to emerge too often. Despite the tightness of the wardrobe, the abyss of not being able to see the palms of my own hands in any detail, I don't often emerge. Here I can breathe easily. It isn't cold, despite the layer of mold covering the sides. There are no mosquitoes, as there are outside. There's no babbling, no unanswered cries: no one deafens you. I should also admit that I actually have more space than those who live outside. But that isn't what's important. What's important to me is that I can see without being seen.

Things become more complicated when there are visitors. Then, up to five of us must be squeezed into the wardrobe.

And when there's a party, it's even worse: above, inside, underneath the wardrobe, all of us, the naked ones selected to be hidden. Naturally, there are plenty of other nooks and crannies intended for storing naked ones, the result being that there are always just as many visitors as there are those in hiding. But whenever I have company in my wardrobe, I do everything possible to make sure nobody notices the hole through which I can see out, my window. I fill the hole with wax, and remain in the dark, like everybody else, trying to sleep so time is consumed quickly, like a quick-burning log.

What would become of us without the wardrobe? Without the lofts, the attics, the alcoves and cellars, without the pantries, storerooms, and cabinets?

Where would they hide us?

It's easy to explain why some of us don't simply go outside when there's a party. Or why they don't send us to someone's house: no one wants to see naked ones in the street, much less in their own homes. And *we* don't want them to see us either. The thought horrifies us, causing panic, fear, shivers down our spines, not exactly because we're terrified of going around naked, but because they themselves, those from outside, seem to be the terrified ones, and do everything possible to terrify *us*, attacking us in all manner of ways. The fear we experience is due entirely to the imminence of these attacks; we're never able to tell for certain what sly tricks, what state-of-the-art inventions they will employ against a recent captive. And as they're so resourceful when it comes to creating increasingly refined instruments of torture, aimed at a perfect conjunction of the most prolonged exasperation and the most agonizing pain, we, experienced in this condition of pain by a remote tradition, understand that not being able to anticipate what form of torture we will be submitted to involves a further form of torture, perhaps a thousand times greater; for this very ignorance forces us to imagine, live, and suffer a hundred times all forms of torture, possible or impossible, that our fancy is able to apprehend. It's a perpetual fever, present even in our dreams; as if every minute of our lives were spent trying to predict the exact manner in which we are going to die, with the added cruelty of knowing that whatever death should befall us will be equally horrible, with no possibility of it being sweet or natural. Of course, this absurd purpose—that of trying to guess what horrible form of death we will encounter—is in itself a horrible way to die. But, in our case, if only we were able to know in advance the method and apparatus used by our torturers and have some idea of the impending pain, we could familiarize ourselves with this pain, with the method, the apparatus, and it's possible that at the crowning moment of the torture, the executioners would be confronted with the timid rictus of a bitter smile, paradoxical, but a smile nonetheless, as if we were thinking out loud: "I knew it would be this pain and no other." And this would imply a victory, relative of course, over the executioner and the pain itself. And given that those living outside this house are permanently clothed, even when they sleep, we sense another, equally dubious, victory; we sense that in some respects they are just as vulnerable as we are, why wouldn't they be? Naked and clothed, we harm each other mutually. Whatever the case, our humble victory confirms the fact that the nakedness of our double sex intimidates, oppresses, depresses, irritates, and distresses them to the point of another kind of pain: hatred.

Hatred, which is the worst pain of all.

And so when they see us in the street, they smile nervously, at first; they cross and uncross their arms; the most peculiar expressions pass over their faces, it's almost comical. Some run to hide their wives and children, somewhat pointlessly, since the wives and children reappear, looking down from their windows, while the older children watch everything from up on the rooftops, armed with slings and pebbles, accompanied by their cats, and occasionally taking part in the insults with the approval of their parents, who, while pretending to ignore them, understand that it's beneficial for their offspring to begin training early in the difficult art of tormenting naked ones. There are women who have been known to spur their husbands on from their balconies, who make suggestions, sparking original ideas intended to increase the rigors of the torture. The older ones, the grandmothers—those ailing from nostalgia and rheumatism—still harbor within their bodies the spontaneous capacity to blush ardently, not precisely out of pity for the captives, or shame for themselves and their grandchildren, but rather with the fires of authentic pleasure. Some recover years of their lives, appearing rejuvenated, asking for the time; they seem more at home in their bodies, and their hearts respond. Others forget their aches and pains altogether. The lame leap to their feet and begin to walk; the ill-tempered smile; the inactive begin to knit and sing vigorously; the apathetic stick their fingers in their mouths like little girls, and begin to dance. We know of one old granny who was so stimulated by the tale of persecution she overheard her neighbors discussing that she recovered the sight she'd lost some years before and was able to thoroughly enjoy a torture session she had the good fortune to witness, sharing her own highly animated impressions. Then she went blind again, but with the contentment and dignity of one who has seen everything in life and is no longer concerned with seeing anything more. Still others, the eldest among them, would die on the spot, splayed out peacefully, with smiles of a kind of dubious beatitude twisting their lips. In short, the positive responses of these limp and ancient bodies to each execution were so satisfactory that the very doctors who lived among the clothed ones did not hesitate to recommend unanimously the torture of a naked one as a surefire remedy for rheumatism, for example, as well as for intestinal obstruction, numbness, asthma, low blood pressure, hair loss, kidney or gallstones, the flu, loss of hearing, hysterics, and, most importantly, boredom, which is a serious condition and fatal to those in the later stages of life, because it does away with hope, and without hope no decrepit body can survive.

However, the infallibility of these medical opinions was brought into question when one of the clothed ones' most distinguished men of science decided to organize an unrivaled torture session, aimed at recovering the health of his mother (who was suffering from a case of hopelessness), and for that purpose, he sought out the most enlightened torturers, checked facts, and consulted evidence, gathering advice and suggestions—from the type of chair and position from which his mother should witness the suffering, the alignment of the stars, the chants and cheers of the crowd, the presence of cats or absence of dogs, to the colors (black, red, and violet) of the gown in which they would forcibly "clothe" the naked one (an original touch, never before conceived), and the colors (pure white and sky blue) of the torturers' garb—all with the aim of producing something memorable, something that went far beyond an ordinary torture session, a perfect assembly of parts, an unsurpassably affecting pain, with the unfortunate result that the so frequently refined process was a resounding failure. For it transpired that the scientist's mother died, and more from disappointment at the method of torture employed than from pleasure. "Isn't there any other way you could torment him?" she asked, before adding: "Damn you all, we're running out of ideas." Afterwards, as she expired, she exclaimed: "Unless we correct this, it won't be long before these naked ones begin choosing their own form of pain, rubbing our faces in the disgrace of their two restless sexes!"

As for the younger, unattached women, we know that during these scenes of torture they're in the habit of running their red and quivering tongues across their dry mouths over and over again, their pearly-white teeth biting into the glistening flesh of their lips, as they all stand, leaning slightly, legs slightly parted, continuing to damage their lips, involuntarily, until drawing blood. They land round, solid little blows against their abdomens, running moist fingertips over their erect nipples over and over again, as if to reproduce within their bodies the sensation of the monstrous caress arising from the pain of the naked ones. And we know all of this from the very recollections of the naked ones (those lucky enough to survive and return to us), because before the torture begins, the senses of the prisoners become as taut as harp strings, and they perceive with indelible precision the details of every word and gesture, the beginning and the end of their torment, to later describe it all in the house, amid the tumultuous questioning of their kin.

And so, after locking their families away, vigilant clothed ones (careful and discreet) hurry out to meet with others— usually loners, the elderly, the unmarried—and now in a group, they work themselves up into a terrible rage. They never remain unaffected as we would hope; they throw tantrums, go bright red, turn green and gasp for air; they cross, uncross, and recross their arms like children. "The street is no place for naked ones," they warn, their index fingers raised to the sky; some fling handfuls of mud at us, or sharp-edged stones; others spit at us, shove us as if playing some ball game, lift and bury us, prepare us, in short, for torture, if they happen to be in the mood, that is, because sometimes they'll decide simply to abduct us then and there, hiding us away for months in their luxury stables, where a horse, they claim, has more wits than any of us.

They tied a naked one to the trunk of an elderberry once, and left him there for days, giving him vinegar instead of water to drink, and piercing his skin from time to time with sticks smeared in toxic aloe juice. They hung a sign around his neck, saying: "FOR BEING NAKED," and you can be sure the sign nearly became his epitaph. They urinated on him, threw bucketfuls of baby shit in his face, until he almost suffocated. He was already very old for a naked one, and, once he'd dragged himself back to the house, he suffered from that terrible smell until the end of his days. He himself told us of his misfortunes, shouting that women and children had taken turns bathing him in the urine and feces of cats, which mix together to form the worst kind of filth. They decorated him with crow's feathers, bird's intestines, and rotting fruit. They painted him. They used barbed wire to draw a map of the town on his back, and in the exact location of our house they branded him with red-hot coals. Mournfully, he re-called the insults from the older ones during the night, the obscene remarks. I could hear him from my wardrobe, could see him through my window, wrinkled, reddened from his injuries. The way he narrated his misfortunes, his fundamental agony: his despair, his wide eyes of a rain-drenched cow—gentle, watery, as if grazing on nostalgia—his hooked nose, his long ash-gray hair, his curly beard. But most of all it was the way he recounted his misadventure, with a tearful accent on certain words, on particular gestures, which made me think it was almost as though he were boasting about the events, working himself up into a reverie by reliving every minute detail of his torment. Likewise, those captivated faces of the naked ones—open-mouthed, in complete suspense—who listened, their bodies squeezed together, struggling to move backwards, amid the pain of the weak and small and the protests of the dissenting, who were unable to listen to the tale in comfort. But they all strove to move away, without moving too far away, surely in order to avoid having to smell up close that conspiracy of terrible smells that had soaked into every single one of the old man's pores, into the deepest recess of his soul, moving possibly with the noble but self-interested goal of allowing the old man enough room to breathe, or to ensure he wouldn't drown in his own stench and succumb too soon. Everything made me think that the curiosity of the naked ones was just as strong as their repulsion toward the terrible smell, but whichever way you looked at it, there was no denying that those in this house took secret pleasure in the pain in which they participated, the pain that sooner or later awaited each of them. And in this way they resembled the clothed ones. And how the very pain being described to them might well be one of life's incentives, something rare and distinctive, a means of escaping the everyday; but I rejected this unexpected reflection, considering it perverse, degrading, and inimical to us.

Besides, I didn't think about this incident again until one night during a party, when this old man who smelled of cat feces wound up dying in my wardrobe. He was the last to come in. I recognized him—as did the others in hiding—by his smell, naturally, which kept us awake. But he himself apologized to us, and even went so far as to try encouraging us to tolerate the smell: "You'd better start getting used to it," he said, "not so you can put up with me, but because at any moment this might happen to one of you, and then you'll have to put up with yourself." We heard him laugh, he had that final strength, enough dignity to laugh. "It's nice inside this wardrobe," he said. "As for me, I should never have agreed to go outside." And he added that he had a funny feeling he would die that very night. "I won't be bothering you again," he said, and we thought we heard him begin to expire, that's what we believed, because while a rhythm of clapping hands was erupting outside, his body was becoming stiffer and stiffer, and eventually he said: "It's all over," and then, we could tell that he really was dying, because he surrendered his spirit when the music stopped, and there was a silence as brief as it was complete. That was the first night I slept with the legs of a corpse around my neck, and something extraordinary happened: his death put an end to his terrible smell.

BUT REMEMBERING THE SMELL OF THE CAT FECES MAKES us realize that it's impossible to successfully flee the clothed ones. We would need help from one of them, some woman, for example (that has occasionally happened, one of them has felt compassion, though not very often, and has freed us, or encouraged the others to allow us to return to the house). But, in general, it's useless to flee. We should hope for some good luck: that they might be feeling apathetic, or tired, they might decide to take a nap, or not be in the mood to discover or point us out, to grind us in their inventions, until we disintegrate.

They're organized, and everything suggests that an important part of that organization lies in their resolve to keep us locked inside this house, for all eternity.

Because those who had to leave our house (and managed to return to tell of it) don't wish to go back outside. They have dogs in their service, they say. Spying dogs. Pigeons, whose turns in the sky are incriminating messages. Trained reptiles that watch over our paths. Fish accomplices, with white eyes, eternally illuminated and sweeping over the beaches, like searchlights. Killer falcons, whose first target is the left eye of the naked one pointed out to them; these falcons carry some incredible passengers around their necks, like collars: little blue snakes, elegant but deadly, that enter the ruptured eye at dizzying speed and shred the naked one's brain. And they don't simply possess vigilant hyenas, lions and tigers, but insects too, among which the bees and ants stand out for their irrefutable precision, without taking anything away from the flies and cockroaches, the crickets, the fireflies, the beetles, all generally programed for the task of following, or—if the need arises—to attack en masse, on a single signal of sounds. Other beings—plants— are controlled from a distance by waves of heat: flowers that spit venom, colossal trees, bold stranglers. There are rocks and crystals, located strategically and in possession of a scrutinizing gaze: anything suspected of being a naked one passing before them is carved perfectly into their bodies, as if under the dictate of an invisible chisel. Others are undefined, subterranean, sexless, diurnal and nocturnal beings, intrepid sentinels, who proceed lethally, without warning, propelled by a glimmer of light. Still others, such as the nightingales and swallows, act under the influence of a combination of sounds and colors. They also have enormous lobsters, with five pairs of legs, that allow themselves to be captured alive as food and then attack by pouncing straight at the naked one's throat; and chameleons, they have chameleons, masters of disguise, marvelous eyewitnesses, rapid dissimulators, handsome hypocrites, no naked one manages to discover them—until it's already too late—and parrots that gather information, memorizing the voices of the naked ones exactly, including their accents, and then flying off to repeat every word with honed perfection before our persecutors; and they have sheep, of proven savagery, cleverly camouflaged beneath their weak and gentle appearance; tarantulas, scorpions, mice and rats—avid police—toads, iguanas, and canaries with poisoned feathers that flutter gently before the naked one, too gently, and then alight gently on their shoulders, trained only to allow themselves to be caressed, or to perpetually invite a caressing hand, and butterflies, bear cubs, child soldiers, even donkeys whose braying—apparently innocent—follows precise instructions, and, what's more, they have specimens created by means of persistent vivisections, among them a tortoise-hare, a winged horse, a cow-frog, a cat-bird, a chicken with teeth—which talks, although no one can understand it, for that is one peak the science of the clothed ones still hasn't scaled—and a black rose, with vampire tears like dew, always fresh, luminous, gifted with fangs, as well as a kind of furious ape-fish, antediluvian in appearance, that is unable to bear the presence of any naked ones without killing them and can pursue and kill skillfully underwater or from tree to tree on land due to its unusual nature. In short, our kind says, they have the whole world on their side. They aren't at all good, those clothed ones, and they aren't happy, though many of them dress like clowns and display broad grins painted over their lips.

But we aren't happy either.

And their offenses don't always take the form of torture. Sometimes they decide to put us to work, humiliating us. Washing and scrubbing their toilets. Disinfecting their mattresses. Cleaning and organizing their stables. Brushing the hair of their hogs until they shine. Sweeping their chimneys. Sleeping with their paralytic nonagenarians. Commiserating with them. Walking them through the labyrinths of their recollections. Telling them that yes, yes, we are they, their dearest departed, returned to them. Bathing them in lukewarm water. Scrubbing them, rinsing them, drying them, combing them, scratching them, scouring them. Bedding their senile fatsos. Licking them. Lulling them to sleep. Telling them yes, swearing that yes, yes, we are the women they are dreaming of. Rocking them. Fanning them. Lighting up their pipes, their hearts. Being umbrellas during storms. Forever pushing their wheelchairs. Playing chess with them, and losing. Being a walking stick, a voice, eyes, ears. Listening to them day and night, nodding when they nod, shaking our heads when they do, laughing when they laugh, crying when they cry, holding our tongues when they're silent, dying when they die, buried alive, embracing them, in their pyramidal tombs. Being war toys for children and young men. Pets. Fools. Eternally keeping the idiot of each family company, and being bigger idiots than they are, because that's our lot. We allow them to use us, finally, to meet any necessity: as plates, as candelabras, as vessels, as tables for their food: on our backs they place steaming meat, cutting into it with knives and forks—on our very backs—in spite of our pain and our screams, our blood that mingles with that of their lightly roasted beef, which they then garnish with furious sauces, and season with spicy condiments and vinegar and lemon, smiling, observing how those merciless juices filter into our wounds. They prop their feet up on the napes of our necks, use our nails to pick their teeth, wipe the grease from their lips in our armpits. They run their rough and grimy fingers back and forth through the down of our sexes and yank at our ears, our testicles, our breasts, depending on the audience. They shave our eyebrows. They relieve us of our ears. A hand. A leg. Our noses. They paint us with black and red stripes, like improbable zebras. They force us to dance: on a table, on a brick, on a stone, on top of a carpet of thorns. They make us sing while urinating. And yet, many of the naked ones who never return to the house aren't simply employed for larks and menial tasks, but rather for their strength, or their attractiveness, or some talent. They're sent to till the land, to knit shawls, to build houses, to work with ceramics and gold, to fish or hunt, to buff mirrors and shine shoes, to milk cows, goats, and elephants, to serve as wet nurses, to drug and then stew geese on game days, to go head-to-head during the annual festival of the sacred boar, to chase ducks ridiculously, to live each day as if already dead, until the point of bursting, until they reach old age, uselessness, premature death, sudden death. Many—and this has been confirmed—are simply used as scarecrows, since not all birds are at the mercy of the clothed ones, and they carry on as scarecrows even after their deaths, unfailingly, because their very corpses continue to serve that function. Not even the buzzards have dared to take advantage of a naked scarecrow, for fear of interfering with the clothed ones. And so this is how we find ourselves, stigmatized. They use and abuse us left, right, and center, and then scream for us to go back to the house, because the truth is that they need us alive, they need us and our two sexes and our house, or perhaps solely our nakedness, our remote docility.

There are already infinite accounts of their many offenses.

But to count the years spent under the filth and shame of their punishments I would have to be born and live and die at least some seventy times.

AND YET STILL WE MUST HIDE OURSELVES FOR THEIR visits, to make room. Only when they leave can we all move around, circling with difficulty through the naked tumult—except me, who remains locked away.

Of course the clothed ones behave very differently when they come to visit. They are one thing outside, and another inside the house. I ask myself whether, away from this wardrobe, I am different.

I don't think so.

Or who knows.

Who can know this?

Who?

I'm unable to predict what my attitude or my possibilities would be upon first appearing on the street. I would feel even more naked. Or perhaps for the first time, I would understand my nakedness, and my nakedness would be double, for I would be walking among clothed ones. Imagining myself away from this wardrobe, from my window, is something terrible, as inconceivable as understanding that those outside can seem friendly when inside the house. Their friendliness is hypocritical, naturally. They recognize we are prepared to entertain them, and therefore greet us. We have no names, but they name us, on a whim, depending on the day of the week, the weather. There are some who get a different name every night; others receive their names according to taste, a character quirk, a mood. Sometimes one gets a name that previously belonged to someone else; others possess their own names, irrefutable: the Bald One, the Mute, the One-Armed, the Deaf One, the Cripple, the Blind One, the Hunchback, the One-Eyed, the Dwarf. But there is one eternal name for us all: *Naked*.

Perhaps it's unnecessary to add that it is precisely because of these parties and the clothed ones' visits that we are able to live—or survive. They bring us indispensable milk, grain, bread, fruit, water, and coal for the ovens; but they aren't generous. We're always hungry. We suffer from perpetual hunger, and I can attest that those in this house think of nothing but eating, of meals and more meals, and even more, always more and more, damn them. Nobody here has ever felt full and stopped thinking for even one miserable minute about his or her meals; the dishes, plates, and stew pots sparkle daily due to the enthusiastic licking of our diners when they finish their lunch; every morning, from the moment they wake, those in this house begin anxiously worrying about meals, and this is because many have experienced being left without so much as a mouthful, and have no wish to repeat that misfortune. Desperate episodes occur, therefore, once the visitors have left. Many throw themselves furiously upon a dinner's leftovers, and there is fighting, pulled hair and blood, lamentations, tears, grievances that are never forgotten; and this is because the clothed ones tend to leave their plates almost untouched and because our cooks' seasoning and the quality of the dinners improve noticeably when there is a party. So great if the hungry anticipation that mothers forget their newborn babies; older children forget their mothers and attack them in the fray; friendships are set aside; the sick, the defenseless, roll across the courtyards like abandoned hoops. We know of human remains, the bodies of little boys and girls above all, that scream out a warning of eternal hunger, of the nefarious depths hunger can reach within us; and yet even these truths are ignored, nobody mentions the disappearances, just as nobody remembers, for example, that remote explanation for the lack of animals in this house.

The most frequent visitors often like to get us to fight over a plate of lentils, and they place bets. It's as if the clothed ones' main goal were to keep us perpetually unsatisfied with our meals; it delights them to observe that we think of nothing else. As for me, I suppose I think of other things because I don't care much about food. A lack of bread, I can't deny, is a very serious discomfort, a strain on the body; contemplation is exhausting; I become an authentic yawn; I need sleep, because sleep is another good trick for hunger, our most highly recommended remedy. Yet this isn't a situation I often find myself in. I've managed to accustom myself to the absence of food; I require only the indispensable: water; water. I'm never exposed to meat, which awakens the appetite, and other appetites; I usually partake of juice and vegetables, and milk if I'm lucky. I'm the tallest and thinnest of the naked ones; from my height, when I walk, I am astonished by the tumultuous sea of swirling heads. Discovering me, a visitor once remarked: "Who is this dead man walking?" and burst into peals of laughter. "He has no skin, he's a skeleton," he said, asphyxiated with glee, "he's just one big breathing bone," and he ordered me to come nearer; he was astounded by the size of my head, disapproved of my nails, shuddered at the length of my hair (which reaches my ankles), and he took my hand and led me to his group, who were drinking wine in one of the more secluded courtyards. They didn't stop laughing for a long time, with me in the center, asking whether I'd ever seen myself in a mirror, and ordering one to be brought over. But I told them no, I would never want to look at myself in a mirror, that if they put one in front of my face I would close my eyes, and that's what happened; they put my face in front of a mirror and I closed my eyes, I barely glimpsed something, or someone who, from his place, had no desire to see me either. For neither he nor I want to be introduced by way of any mirror, because it isn't necessary. I don't want confirmation of how this face looks in a mirror, because I know my face by my hands, and my hands by my lips, and am fully aware of my body, my slenderness of a tree branch, my transparency, for I can see my veins and can glimpse my red and white heart, and can also hear the rattle of my bones as I walk; because I know, finally, who I am, a naked one, and know perfectly well that my name is as naked as me. In this I am absolutely different from the rest of the inhabitants of the house, who spend hours in front of mirrors, absorbed in their bodies, in their two sexes, in their eyes, in their hair, into which they impart the most extravagant style and color. For it has come time to confess that our hair is the only sort of clothing we naked ones possess, our only clothes. My hair is a suit. But I don't wrap or unwrap it, dye or bleach it, bunch or pile it, cut or frizz it. I don't praise or despair of it. I wet it, comb it, muss it up, loathe it, I convert it into a mound of thunderbolts, or into a single ball of flame.

The clothed ones also asked me if I wasn't afraid of dying soon, because I was clearly rusting away. "You have no flesh," they said, although later they recognized with astonishment the gleam in my eyes, and commented on it: "We're very surprised by the light there is in each of your eyes," and another voice said: "A distinct light in each eye." "That can't be," said another. "Yes, yes," replied the first, amazed, "they're distinct lights," and another voice, meditatively: "Light, after all, and that could be a danger to us; no naked ones have light in their eyes," but another corrected him: "That depends on the cause, on the fire that feeds it." "I could discover the reason," said another, in a sultry whisper. It was the voice of a woman (for among the clothed visitors there are also women, who tend to wear dark veils covering half their faces, so that only their eyes peer out, large, clear, and shimmering), and they carried on like that for what seemed an eternity, contemplating me from all directions, listening to my heartbeat, pointing out the pallor of my face, the length of my nails, the color of my hair: "Red, red," she above all, running her fingers through my hair over and over again. "Red, red"—almost excited? almost perplexed?—her fingers were as cold as iron but like fire, sinking into the ram's down teeming across my chest and abdomen, the nape of my neck, my back, a down thickening at my navel and falling like a curtain—like another long, thick crop of hair—to the top of my legs, which are absolutely hairless and straight, pale, just like my smooth-skinned face; and this left them stunned, and attracted the hands—cold? aflame?—which now began to knead my calves, while the remaining voices persisted in exchanging impressions, until one of them finally asked:

"How old are you?"

"I'm not sure, but it's likely I'm a hundred years old, or five hundred, or perhaps it has only been a single year since my birth. I've never been able to find out for certain."

"Are you being sincere?" the sultry voice asked.

"Yes," I said. "I believe so."

"You're making fun of us!" yelled one of them, with more admiration than fury, and at that, the naked ones who were lurking and listening in sprang back, because it isn't often that one of our own responds like this to an interrogation; generally we respond only as far as strictly necessary, in monosyllables, without ever meeting the eyes of the clothed one—unless ordered to do so—and without once letting slip the slightest suggestion of our own reasoning, our tiredness, our distance. Being chosen for conversation with clothed ones is rare; the naked ones who enjoy a chat like this, who might have to answer two or three questions—"Are you happy?" "What would you like to be called?"—can feel very satisfied, because this means they have been chosen to indulge one or more clothed ones, and depending on their performance, they stand to earn not one but a number of platefuls of meat, if they please their benefactors, of course, because otherwise they should fear the worst; that they'll be punished and sent—for example—to bring wine from the cellar, and then to carry the full pitcher back to that very same cellar and return the wine to its cask, before decanting more wine from the same cask, and over and over—in an exhaustion of comings and goings—to the point of collapse or the end of the party or the weariness or pity of the clothed ones, or—in the case of an old-timer—until death. They'll be ordered to fetch scouring pads and soap with which to wash and scrub dozens of pairs of feet, sometimes hard and calloused, sometimes soft and pink, but always grouchy and oversensitive. Withstanding shoves and blows, amid fussing and mockery, they repeat this task over and over, despite the fact that the ankles are already perfectly clean and there's no filth left under anybody's nails;. many demand to have their toes sucked for hours, to be fanned, to be carried from place to place upon our backs, to be tickled, to be stared at intently without blinking to the point of tears, and for every blink, for every transgression, there's a ferocious blow with a riding crop or a wooden cane, a red-hot iron, or a sword, which more often than not proves fatal.

When they tried to peer closely at the most hidden secret of my body, I let out a howl of rage, which was neither voluntary nor one that seemed to belong to me, because its tone was as if someone else howled from some other distant place in time. I began to run in search of the wardrobe, sensing that the first impulse of the clothed ones was to come after me—they even ordered that I be detained—but the voice of that same woman who believed she could discover the reason for the gleam in my pupils stopped them, and was in time to overturn the order for my capture (for already various naked arms were extended, intending to apprehend me, surely in order to ingratiate themselves with the clothed ones). "Let him go," she yelled, "he's just a wandering gaze," and then somebody, not her, must have made a crude joke at my expense, for I could hear morbid laughter. The amazement was felt only among the naked ones, who aren't accustomed to seeing one of our own rebel against the visitors; they made way, panting—a furrow of bodies opening up before me—and so I was able to reach the wardrobe and with one tug remove the first drowsy occupant I could lay my hands on and take up a place in the darkness of my whole life, my wardrobe, where nobody has any interest in examining the down of my sexes. Since that occasion I have tried as far as possible not to venture outside again when there is a party, or visitors, in spite of my hunger; I sleep through entire nights and days, hoping I might be wiped forever from the memories of the clothed ones and escape their vengeance, though I am certain that she, the savior, won't be the first to forget me. I'm unable to forget her either, and in the midst of my dreams I continue to live outside, with her, hearing her words, feeling her fingers, suffering them. My dream, my eternal torpor, has transformed her into a living participant of my window, because when I peer out it's as though I were watching her, laughing and twirling naked, as if she were another one of us.

THE CLOTHED ONES ENJOY THEMSELVES WITH GREAT IN-
tensity in our house; they're paradoxical revelers: they arrive sometimes like a fantastic whirlwind, whooping with
excitement, and at other times with heads bowed, as if already repenting of the great error they wish to commit; but
usually they just stomp around, smoking, drinking, and sa-
voring the dishes we lay out on the tables.

During the hors d'oeuvres the clothed women talk to
us about birds and animals, they give us basic lessons in
reading and writing, in a history and geography that be-
longs only to them; they explain to us about addition, sub-
traction, and division, they deliver sermons on health and
behavior, on etiquette—how one should sit or one should
walk, on the need for a balanced diet and for exercise, on
the maternal obligation to breastfeed children up to a certain age, in short, a whole incongruous world of advice and
theories that, due to our way of life, are of very little use to
us. They show us large pictures of animals and gloat over

our astonishment; our questions make them laugh until their eyes well up with tears. "But what imbeciles they are," they say, showing us enormous landscapes, where hundreds of seals can be seen spread across the beach, tightly packed, like us. "And this is a tarantula," they say, "and this is a tortoise that's been basking in the sun for four hundred years." They help us finally (with each and every one of their conclusions) to understand that if we are where and how we are, it's because this is where and how we're supposed to be, because we could be no other way, and should therefore try to live our lives as happily as we can, and nothing more, for the sun and the planets spin solely around their heads, and always have done.

The clothed men, for their part, talk frequently about the great war they're preparing for, about the weapons and instruments that will make them an invincible force in the world. They talk about a fabulous trap their most important scientists are working on, designed solely for a naked one who escapes from the house—they smile grimly and a collective shiver passes over us—but they continue to lecture us about the war, because all they want is war, although, of course, while preparing for war they can still distract themselves by torturing us, in order to simulate a small great war. For the officers, the men of science, of laws and letters, and the more practical ones, can speak of nothing but war, even while they shit, because they dream of war, they wake with their arms wrapped around it, and, occasionally, with the aim of shaking us to attention, they mention the fearsome trap awaiting anyone who tries to escape the house. "Someday," predict the scientists, in lowered voices, "we'll be able to shrink this house. We'll turn it into a doll's house," and then they burst into laughter, and we ask ourselves whether it's possible they could achieve this. It's possible, we conclude, and yet we continue to turn it over in our minds, like a nearby nightmare. Finally, they leave the house with a great desire to return. You can read it on their faces and in the way they look back over their shoulders; and yet these pleasant memories of our house disappear as soon as the door closes behind them. Perhaps they're feeling the pangs of an enormous envy at our naked way of life, an envy with no foundation, it would appear to me, for they themselves could, if they chose to, take off their clothes and walk around like this, naked, in their homes, or in the streets, if they so desired, when the weather is good, for example, and the sun is out. But they would never do this; even inside our house they only ever tend to get half undressed; they always keep something on—a shirt, a pair of trousers, their shoes. Maybe they don't want to look and feel similar to us, because apart from our two sexes we differ from them only in our total inability to put on clothes. I've never been able to discover where this inability came from, what its origin is, and if it really is an inability, a virtue, a custom, or a necessity. I've heard it said that an item of clothing would set fire to our skin, but I'm not certain of that, I haven't witnessed it myself; instead I heard this claim made one evening, without being able to distinguish

the face from which it came. I remember the voice, vehement, terrified; he assured us that he'd happened upon a
naked one who was in the midst of trying on the garments
of a visitor, saying that no sooner had the man slipped his
body into the last piece of clothing than he collapsed, en-
gulfed in flames, and disappeared. The possibility was then
raised that the clothing in question may have belonged to
an amusing prankster who'd prepared that fiery trap aim-
ing to tempt and torment the first incautious naked one
who decided to try on clothes, that the owner of the pyro-
maniac clothing was probably nothing more than a pyro-
maniac himself. Or that all the garments of every visiting
clothed one might contain a secret device that, on being
taken off their customary bodies, even for an instant, are ac-
tivated to explode, to burn, and to kill, at the slightest hint
of unknown skin. The science of the clothed ones seems
very advanced to us; yet even so, we discussed the possibility of a coincidence; perhaps an act of chance had set fire
to the clothes, or no doubt a burning torch fell onto the
naked one's clothing, or onto the naked one himself at the
crucial moment of putting on these clothes. For my part, I
guessed at a further possibility: that the witness, obeying
strict instructions, invented the story about the incendiary
clothing to dissuade anyone intending to put on clothes in
the hope of incorporating themselves—clothed—into the
world of the clothed ones, concealing their two sexes. It
was never established which of these possibilities was the
truth, or if none of them was, or if each and every one was

on the mark. The fact is, as far as we can tell, nobody has any intention of living among the clothed ones; there are no reliable reports of naked ones ever wanting or having wanted to disguise themselves as clothed ones. None of our ancestors wore clothes. Of that there is a clear record in the naked ones' cemetery—the Naked Cemetery, as the clothed ones refer to it—where each tombstone is engraved with the resounding inscription: "I, NAKED."

The cemetery is a large blanket of pitch-black earth, dotted with willows and boulders, at the back of the house; it's the only territory belonging to us that can be found outside our walls. If one day we manage to leave this house unpunished, without being pursued, it will be because we are dead. Only in death can we reach a place with no roof, beneath the clouds, in the wind, under the earth, which is as naked as we are. Only by dying.

The oldest tomb is made of weathered stone (by which its relative antiquity can be appreciated) and is positioned at the exact center of the cemetery. It is the only one that bears a different inscription. Most of the words are impossible to read, because the symbols can barely be made out, are only traces, like memories of letters; only the words found at the tombstone's very center can be read, and I'm given to understand that even these can be deciphered only with great effort, because several of the marks must be intuited, guessed at. The tombstone reads: "(AN)D SH(E) DAR(ED) (TO) LI(V)E (NA)KED."

It's more than likely that the first woman—the first tomb-stone—was also the first owner of the house we inhabit to-day. We cannot imagine with whom she might have lived here. Nor do we know who carved that inscription on the tombstone, or whether it was the woman herself who, be-fore her death, ordered the engraving from strangers. What-ever the case, there is not a single remnant inside the house that can reveal anything about this woman or the house's origins. Someone, or something, must be responsible for the disappearance of the past, for having pulverized any utensil or presence, sound, or image that might express the memory of anyone or anything. For example, the things in this house don't appear to belong to any time, or to anyone; it's as though they were made in fragments: one piece one distant evening, and another today, right now, at this very moment. Of course, the foundations of the house are old; many of the walls are crumbling to bits, there is damp, and yet our visitors—those very same clothed ones, our aggres-sors in the street—won't allow the house to collapse; they maintain it, check and reinforce its underpinnings, they permanently sustain its frame, from outside, without com-ing in. Many mornings we've been woken by the sound of meticulous hammering, the scraping of trowels, the groan-ing of the increasingly complex network of ropes and joists that struggle to keep the house from falling apart. This is because they are straightening the roofs; it's because they are reinforcing the only door that remains unsealed (all the other doors and windows have been boarded up from outside); it's because they're realigning the eaves, bolstering the facade, making it impenetrable, adding more fossils and stones to its recesses. It's because they're locking us deeper and deeper inside our prison.

Maybe this house was also a prison for its first inhabitant, why not? Or maybe that woman lived alone and happy. If someone else had lived here intimately with her, there would be evidence of this on another tombstone; but the first tombstone stands alone, positioned in the center, at a considerable distance from the others, which are sequential, identical. We believe, therefore, that the first woman lived alone, completely. She must have lived among the clothed ones to begin with, and then absolutely alone, in the warmer half of her enormous house, where she would have discovered that she had two sexes—as much man as woman—and decided to become permanently naked. It's difficult to imagine that among the clothed ones there could have been someone free and resolved enough to accompany her day and night. Perhaps some of them would have spent an evening with her, passionately, and then the woman had children, it's possible, or she procreated with herself and then died, and her children with two sexes decided to live as she had lived, and maybe the first children produced their own successors, or maybe not, who can know that? Or maybe the woman's successors were simply acquaintances, or friends, or strangers who decided to perpetuate this nakedness. Who can say? We can't know anything for sure. We believe and don't believe. We guess and guess and guess. We only know, for example, that the children of naked ones are usually fathered by clothed ones, but this, of course, doesn't matter to them, the clothed ones, and much less to the naked mothers; in any case, in this house of two sexes nobody has yet dared to procreate by themselves. We haven't witnessed it, at least, and we don't know if things were like this before, we cannot guess. We prefer to think that previously, among our ancestors, there can't have existed this sense of abandonment we feel today, this eternal defeat, this staggering debasement, this inevitable enslavement in which we've allowed ourselves to be plunged.

Mothers stay with their children during the first years, and then, when the children can—apparently—defend themselves, they release them, they cast them into the naked tumult, and forget them. I've seen mothers who despair at having to provide for their children, letting out huge yawns while contemplating them. I never knew if this was because they were racked by exhaustion and fatigue, or out of hunger, a cyclopean desire to devour their young. In any case, these are the same mothers who take responsibility for explaining to them—with beatings, yelling, and gestures—the world into which they've arrived. Otherwise, the majority of us (and even our mothers themselves) would never have been able to survive. For my part, I don't know which of all these women—who wander in circles throughout the house, and whose troubled eyes sometimes occupy the miniature abyss of my window—is my mother. It's likely she's still alive. As for my father, he could be a naked one, or a clothed one; in either case his absence is the same. I know, from the sporadic comments of one or other of the elders who remembers, that an old woman snatched me from my mother's arms the moment I was born, and held me pressed tightly against her, my head between her breasts, my body sheltered beneath her hair, and she didn't allow anyone to touch or look at me for years. In other words, she defended me from death until she herself died. And yet, according to these same offhand comments, I continued to behave as though the old woman were still alive, hiding from everyone and everything, fleeing even from their looks, from the trembling hands that were sometimes extended toward me; and when I was finally able to find my place inside my wardrobe, my respite, nobody could say they had ever seen me defenseless before the eyes of anyone, not a single time.

And so I grew. I don't know if I have siblings. I don't want to know. It makes no difference. In this house, we are all alone. In this house nobody can trace a direct link to their predecessors, dead or living; nobody knows where or how or why or whether their siblings, cousins, or grandparents still breathe. The old-timers almost never talk about themselves, or about us, and when they do, they skirt nervously around each topic, always with an incredulous gaze straying toward the empty plates, as if awaiting anxiously—though with little hope—the weight and presence of more food.

When I tried to coax something about my past from the

elders, I learned of nothing but the abduction and the old lady who defended me from death. And when I ventured to ask about the pasts of these same elders, about their lives—and as such about ourselves, about our past—it was useless, absurd; they confessed nothing because they know nothing, except that they themselves don't ask about it either. They know only what we all know: that we appeared wandering among the naked tumult with two sexes (some more man than woman and others more woman than man), and that on the other side of the door only death awaits. Very occasionally, the elders talk among themselves in low voices, but they only say what other elders in other corners and at other times have always said. They recall the cemetery, for example, a favorite topic, the first tombstone, torture in the street, and then they go silent, chewing on invisible mouthfuls, to strengthen their jaws, I presume, to be able to devour more when the fleeting opportunity arrives, or perhaps to have an excuse to remain eternally silent, shrugging their shoulders.

The oldest of the naked ones is a gruff, bald giant who invariably sits in the most hotly contested corner—next to one of the largest kitchens—from which he can grab a piece of something simply by extending one of his big hairy hands. He's like a statue made of dark marble, covered by what is surely the longest and thickest beard that's ever existed in the entire history of this house. Occasionally, he's approached by groups of visitors who set about enthusiastically examining him: first they move aside the long, ash-gray train of his beard—which always rests between his stonelike legs—and observe him closely, with cries of jubilant panic, and then they stimulate him, rousing him with two or three sharp raps, as if knocking at a door (though the mere stupefaction of the clothed ones constitutes a stimulus for the old-timer). Next they measure him, weigh him, issuing unanimous exclamations; they slap the old man on the back, as if congratulating him, before carefully drawing his beard back across his most essential union, and finally they interrogate him, amid laughter, about his self-amorous encounters—never wishing to procreate, he has always withdrawn at the crucial moment; they encourage and investigate him, without ever disrespecting him, without ever unsettling him with a severe look, for it so happens that this enormous bald elder is like a religion, the grandiose shell of what was once a titan, a colossal relic, peremptorily instituted by the clothed ones, a bountiful scrap heap who must be maintained and obeyed—an extraordinary pastime, the most naked of distractions, a savage celebration sometimes achieving miracles of happiness for the women with veiled faces, for as they themselves put it, this old man is our tender barbarity to enjoy, the most beautiful game of love that continues to live despite his age, a volcano, a beating heart, so they reward the old man with two or three plates of raw meat and bid him affectionate farewells, with more vigorous backslapping, as if encouraging him to remain alive until the next visit, the next necessity, the next use. He is protected, one of the few.

They call him Jesús.

And just like Jesús, the majority of old-timers can be found dispersed in the corners closest to the kitchens, all leaning against the walls, panting, as if attempting strategically to protect their backs—pink and slavering seals, huge, small, wrinkled, and hoarse. Damp, despicable seals. Seals and seals and more seals.

And the attempts the old-timers make are desperate: the faces and the performances—fastidious, or comic, or tragic, but always obscene—which they devise with the sole aim of attracting the sympathies, or at least the attentions, of the visitors. At these times an antediluvian din can be heard, like a tremendous hieroglyph, a flurry of accents, and if it weren't for the fact that the clothed ones occasionally ordered the elders to be quiet, nobody would be able to understand anybody else, or even understand themselves, and this entire house would end up oblivious and obliterated. In these cases, we first seek to kindly persuade the elders to be quiet, and if this doesn't work, we gag them, or we tie them up if they still have the strength to walk. Many expire in this way—already weakened by their efforts, it's the final shock—or else they go red with rage, with intense resentment, because we won't allow them to yell and perform the little theatrical number which they've surely been preparing weeks in advance, believing they might finally pull off that great coup that would convert them overnight into favorites, just like Jesús.

Only the young care or worry about the parties for any reason other than eating. They await that extraordinary coincidence that will distract them from the house, from the eternal routine of identical mornings, evenings, and nights; from feeling themselves always the same within these identical walls. And as they are frequent participants in the games and capers organized by the visitors to distract themselves, the young always have an opportunity for a dissonance that sets their hearts beating in reverse, a dangerous amusement, mysterious and bittersweet, keen-edged, even if this amusement does so often end up proving fatal; for all of these reasons, they await the parties with an eagerness perhaps akin to that of the clothed ones when they decide to come visit us.

The young are fascinated by the notion that our skin is identical to that of the clothed ones, and they're even more astonished to learn—and finally accept—that the big difference between us resides in the fact that we have one more sex, and that the clothed ones come from outside, whereas we, on the other hand, are and always will be found inside the house. Our expeditions outside are very brief, dark misfortunes that may well lead to death: those selected to leave run this huge risk, but they must go, with no complaints, to carry out the errands for the house; otherwise the risk would be run by all of us. And the truth is that the clothed ones are absolutely delighted by the fact that, from time to time, one of us must cautiously open the door and appear all of a sudden, startled, and take a first step—reluctantly—

and another, ashen, and another, panic-stricken, and another, on the verge of fainting, and face the anguish of an unknown street on tenterhooks, the humiliating appeal for supplies, the terrifying risk of torture. This is the reason they never bring us everything we need, the indispensable provisions on which we survive. Except for the final definitive departure, to the cemetery, we cannot go outside unless we're wide-eyed with terror, chattering with cold, pleading with fate that the clothed ones might grow tired of attacking us and simply shrug their shoulders and spit in our faces, degrading us, but ultimately giving us what we need.

THERE IS ONLY ONE NIGHT EACH MONTH WHEN ONE OF us may go outside without the risk of torture, and the chosen one is a woman. They call her the Bird. She leaves the house without any trepidation and goes silently to a small corner of the cemetery where she cultivates flowers. She talks to them, turning the black earth with her fingers, she waters them; sometimes it sounds as if she's urinating on them, sometimes as if she's crying, sometimes as if she's laughing, and she also sings: all the sounds that pour from her are like water; and sometimes she's silent, but even this can be heard: it's the sound of hands and earth.

During each of these nights, the clothed ones spread out like plaster figurines, sprite-like, in hats and raincoats, all around the cemetery. Some make themselves comfortable on top of enormous rocks, wide and flat like stages; others, the more agile, climb to the top of the strongest willows. But the majority continue to circulate, primed and attentive, around the edges of the cemetery, following and observing each movement the Bird makes inside the garden—when she cries, sings, laughs, and when she urinates on her flowers, like someone praying. For the clothed ones, it must prove very exciting to kill time in this way, trying to distinguish the long, tranquil movements of this naked one. "There she is," they say, and another voice: "No, no she's over there," and another: "She's over that way." "She's over this way." "No." "Yes." "Of course she is." "She isn't, I swear it." And in the absolute silence of the house—a silence identical to the one inside the cemetery—we can make out their words clearly, because there isn't a party in our house, because none of our voices are sounding; because it's as though even our hearts have stopped. And we are unable to understand the reason why the clothed ones express so much interest on this one specific night, the epicenter of which appears to be nothing more than a guessing game: in what precise location is the naked one currently leaning to water her flowers, and what is she saying to them, and how many times has she circled the garden, how many yawns, and what is she singing? Is she crying? Laughing? "No, no, at this precise moment she's just started to pee." As if someone were praying.

We know that the clothed ones who try hardest to find the naked one are those who celebrate her most when they arrive back at the house; they're the ones who allow her to tend her flowers, the ones who prevent (by way of warnings among their own) any attempts at aggression. It's possible, we think, that during these nights the clothed ones place heavy bets upon the appearances of the Bird. Whoever spots her first, pointing her out on the most occasions, is the winner and earns the highest prize (the Bird herself) upon the next visit, because otherwise we just can't explain such dogged determination to discover her, so much arguing and jostling over this subject. It even seems that in the bitterest disputes they turn to a referee, a judge, a mediator; in short, it's impossible to decipher the subtleties of the recreations of the clothed ones. It's also very likely that, as in some big, gruesome game, the clothed ones are simply tempting this naked one to escape, to flee into the night—a dark bird—and that everyone would then chase after her, with whoever managed to capture her keeping her for life, like some kind of crown of laurels. Kill her. Chain her up. What would the winner do with her? How can we know? Set her free? Stuff her and put her up on a marble wall, like a hunting trophy? Tie her to the oak leg of a bed and then asphyxiate her in that bed's climactic moment? What would they do? Bury her? How can we know? What is clear is that we don't know anything. We continue to be in the dark about why the clothed ones have allowed the Bird to go outside one night each month without being pursued, and, what is even more unheard of, to plant flowers, urinate on them, talk to them, sing, laugh, and cry.

Whatever the reason, I've heard the Bird say that instead of flowers she would like to plant vegetables, that tending flowers is her most excruciating torture.

AND I'VE SEEN SEVERAL CLOTHED ONES NAKED, I'VE
touched them sometimes, stretching a hand out from my
wardrobe during the most tremendous nights of partying,
when the world is spinning before my door and window,
when the confusion is at its greatest, as is my curiosity to es-
tablish whether we really are different, or whether they simply keep their other sex very well hidden. Despite the fact
that they always leave on an item of clothing so as not to be
confused with us, I have been able to examine their pores up
close, the irises of their eyes, their tongues, their nails, their
ears. I had the freedom to contemplate them long before
one of them became aware of my presence—my eyes, my
head, my long and bony hands—and then summoned me,
subjecting me to his scrutiny, backed by others of his kind.
Ever since they accidentally discovered me I've realized
that I will never again be able to tolerate the clothed ones'
merciless examination of me, selecting me from among
the inhabitants of this house, exasperating me perilously.

In their eyes I'm able to read what the street might be, and in their gestures and words, I feel as though I were sniffing their armpits, the intestinal joy awakened in them by potential torture, and a great chill runs down my spine: hatred, fear.

They were astonished by the extraordinary pallor of my face and the extraordinarily red color of my hair, my waxy fingers, the red ram's wool that covers my back and abdomen and chest, my legs that glow in the milky light of the torches. They were astonished I was able to speak and respond and refute.

As for me, I discovered that they have only one sex, and so we are superior; we have to be, though we never consider this. In any case, we must be a horrible contrast for them. A grimace on two legs, each pointing in different directions. The two legs flee in terror, splitting the center; the grimace is amphibian—a double or deformed spirit?—and the center, the trunk, comes apart. We are the heart of a pig inhabiting a young girl. I have two sexes, like all those who live inside this house, yet only I seem convinced of our superiority, and, what's more, I feel fear and hatred, an inevitable desire to kill, every which way, and then give up.

Now I remember that when I fled from the clothed ones I was not only able to hear the voice of the savior—her voice, the one belonging to her, which said: "Let him go, he's just a wandering gaze"—but that I also heard another voice: "Let's hope one morning we see you on our street." I heard that as well, through the laughter, like a cruel threat, why hadn't I remembered this before? And I recall how on that occasion I experienced as much rage as dejection, as much hatred as shame. Two opposing sentiments that shook me like an authentic red-hot metal blade bifurcating my thoughts. Two desires: to kill or flee (to flee in horror, begging forgiveness for the simple fact of being what I am, to surrender, to hand myself in).

The first desire, to kill, means my ruin; it is related to the desire that they do finally discover me in the street one day and capture me. Then, I would have the opportunity to attack them, strengthened by the same fury that we inside the house use against each other over a plate of meat; and this act would be fatal, for surely I would be unable to kill, though I'd certainly do some damage. I'd bury my nails in their necks, tearing apart their veins without ever letting go. I have nails that are strong and sharp, I file them daily, without needing to leave this wardrobe. I protect them like a warrior burnishing his weapons, because of my certainty that sooner or later I'll have to go out onto the street, as a representative for those in the house and their needs; but I won't beg for anything, rather I shall defend myself. I haven't confessed to any other naked one that I have this mysterious inclination to defend myself; it would seem strange to them; they'd be fearful. They wouldn't understand, because when they're out in the street, the naked ones pretend to flee if they're pursued, until they're captured. Then they meekly submit to torture; some have even collaborated with the clothed ones, so that the torture goes perfectly, with no mistakes, and it can all be over quickly, hopefully without the most fearsome result: death. Not me. I want to defend myself, I want to surprise them before I die.

As for the other desire—to flee, to give in—it would cause me the most suffering, because it wouldn't differentiate me much from the other naked ones; it would force me to endure that other facet of myself, absolute fragility. This other desire reminds me constantly of the voice of the woman who subjected me to her interrogation, who ultimately prevented her companions from demanding my capture. When I become aware of this desire, I feel ashamed of myself and close my eyes, and yet the desire persists: to hand myself over, it's true, but in the sense of being protected forever, being defended—for example—by that same woman, eternally, by her, or by any other clothed one who removes me permanently from this house and the surrounding streets, from the daily threats, the lack of bread, from this perennial exhaustion that sometimes has me believing my blood is evaporating, that I'm nothing but an absurd collapsing delirium. It is the desire to flee not so much from the clothed ones as from myself: never to face myself again, never to question myself, never to ponder over our history and condition, to be just another favorite so as not to suffer. To flee and submit myself, unconditionally: to please. To please more, even more, and to hurl myself into the fire, smiling. I can assume, therefore, that this desire has traces of a peculiar cunning: it does not consider my ruin, but instead the absence of a part of me; and this makes it abhorrent. It offers me salvation at the cost of enslavement; there will be no more thinking or suffering. I shall eat from the finest platters, and sleep and be at peace, though ultimately I shall have to answer for my actions with a submissive face before my master. I would resign myself; I would turn away from my very self, so as not to question. I would ignore my naked shadow.

Whichever desire comes to pass, whichever prevails, I know that above all else in the world I must never allow the cooks—who are practically the representatives of the clothed ones in this house, who keep order, silencing the elders and capturing the women and children indicated by the visitors—I will never allow these cooks to cut my nails. I've told them that I let my nails grow in order to better seek out cockroaches. My nails are like prongs, I tell them, I use them to burst lice, bisect beetles, startle flies. I've used all sorts of arguments to demonstrate how in my total confinement I am absolutely harmless and defenseless before the world—my tortoise-like incapacity—and I've managed to fool them completely. They think I am the gentlest of calves on this earth, a worm in the grass, a hummingbird.

For the cooks aren't very wise, though they pretend to be, with their glowering brows, their bloodstained aprons, their hands laden with food, inquisitors, with their henchman's boots, their tall white hats, the pungent grease that stains their shirts; of course they aren't wearing any of this clothing, but it's as if they were, which is worse. Either they aren't wise, or they simply don't notice the premeditated details, or don't care about complying fully with the orders of the clothed ones. They're far too preoccupied with cooking—the meals are exacting, stewed to perfection—to also have to keep up with policing responsibilities. Why go to all that trouble? At the end of the day, they're happy cooks, they can eat what they like. They receive and store the supplies, even measuring out each naked one's meal in accordance with their own frame of mind. They are, in short, the most respected of the naked ones; they rule on who is right when there are confrontations, which is why they don't spend too much time wondering about why a single inhabitant of the house does not wish to have his nails trimmed. And yet the clothed ones' orders leave no room for doubt: no naked one is to be allowed long fingernails. The ingenuous cooks attribute this order to a principle of cleanliness, akin to oral hygiene. But I don't think that's it. The clothed ones are cautious. I remember all too well the mistrust they demonstrated on discovering me—they were suspicious even of the gleam in my eyes. That's why they alert the cooks to any trace of weapons, whatever they may be. Their consciences are not clear, and with good reason. The cooks obey, to the best of their limited understanding. Two of them kept a fairly relentless watch over me for a number of weeks after my escape from the clothed ones.

Occasionally, the cooks take unexpected walks, to keep a closer eye on us; this is how they can see which of us is ill, or who is dreaming.

A cook—it's true—is like any other clothed one. It's generally they who decide who should leave the house, to carry out the errands. While I must admit that they very rarely select a woman (and never a child) to face the street, they never choose from among themselves either. They watch each other's backs, only ever instructing the nearest and dearest in their profession.

They're cautious.

And when, all of a sudden, they open the door to the wardrobe, believing they can surprise me (I've already seen them through my window), they carefully inspect my face, they sniff around every corner of the wardrobe, and then smile, dubiously. Once again, I adopt the face of an idiot, that which I should have shown when the clothed ones interrogated me. And if they consider my nails with distrust, I repeat that I use them to tear down spiderwebs, to scrape at the most deeply hidden filth in my dwelling. In order to test me, they've occasionally sent me to do battle with the chaos in the kitchens, a flash cleansing of pots, pans, and stoves, and they smile in satisfaction when I inform them that the work is done. They admire my stature, it fascinates them to stand and compare their fat bellies with my wiry silhouette; then they forget about me, and I remain hidden. Thus, I've managed to keep my nails from their scissors, without anyone suspecting that, in reality, I carry knives on my hands. For nobody in this house has ever stopped to think that with my nails I could pierce anybody's skin. It's likely no one thinks me capable of doing something like that; it's likely their heads are simply unable to grasp the notion that a naked one could kill another naked one with his nails, or, what's even more incredible, that a naked one could kill a clothed one.

It's true that besides the usual deaths from torture, other deaths occur in this house, but they're always surreptitious, and the victims are generally children, weak women, collapsed elders. They die by strangulation, or by asphyxiation produced by the multitude of naked bodies jostling and crowding each other for food. Yet no one has ever attacked anybody openly. If we don't love, we don't hate anyone either. Like furious caged animals, we pulse in expectation of the arrival of food.

And the weakest die.

Of course, those killed by torture are immediately transported to the cemetery in the presence of the clothed ones. But the surreptitious dead are usually devoured, and this is something we are all aware of. However, when these surreptitious dead can't be dismembered and then consumed or completely disappeared (anyone caught doing this would be put to death), the corpses arrive at the cemetery in pieces, incomplete. Yet nobody says a word about it. Most act as innocent as a river. As for the direct witnesses, the discovery of butchered bodies must appear perfectly natural to them, much like the deaths of the sick, or of an old-timer, for example. Why make a fuss? From time to time the cooks become secretly annoyed, for they're the only ones authorized to act as gravediggers, and it pains their souls to have to lug those body parts, open up pits, and then fill them in—work that has little or nothing to do with the kitchen and that must be performed in the chill of night, after having been subjected to the approval, rage, and admonishment of vigilant clothed ones. But they conceal this unhappiness, so as not to fall foul of their masters, and because it's still an honor—if only relative—to be able to leave the house without any fear of reprisal. No more than two cooks per corpse may go out. I've noticed that when the surreptitious deaths increase, there is meat in the house for almost everyone. The most innocent among us, the majority—who don't know, or don't want to know, anything about these deaths—suppose the abundance of meat on their plates is the result of good fortune, or because—as I've heard them suggest as they eat greedily—even the cooks have days when they're in a good mood. But I don't think so. I'll never trust in the cooks' good moods. Rather, I believe what's happened is that it's simply occurred to the cooks to serve naked flesh to those innocent naked ones, to avoid a burial, and as a reprisal for their enforced role as gravediggers, as revenge upon us—upon those who have never killed, much less desired the flesh of naked ones—and for the tremendous subterranean joke the clothed ones have played on them; for it's as though with each burial the clothed ones were reminding the cooks: "Yes, you are the chosen, the representatives, but you'll never be anything more than naked ones, not just servants to us, but servants to your dead, and not just those who agonized under torture, but the inferior, the eviscerated."

It's possible, therefore, that many in this house have at some point tasted the flesh of a father, mother, or sibling without noticing, or without wanting to notice. Who knows? Who can know this? And if the cooks are our police, as well as our gravediggers, it's also possible that they frequently are the cause of these surreptitious deaths. Many are quick-tempered, issuing death threats against anyone unfortunate enough to interrupt their work, or anyone who disturbs them by pleading for more and more food. They refrain, however, from disturbing the favorites: the Bird, for example, can be provided with a good plate of meat at any hour of the day; Jesús, the oldest naked one, can eternally extend his hand and find his bowl full, as can other favorites. But they're a minority. Most are a sickly, expectant, starving multitude.

In any case, the naked ones' hunger has never been so bad that one has decided—of his own accord, or with others—to kill and eat a cook, for example. That is a point the naked ones' hunger has never reached.

They're cautious, the cooks, just like the clothed ones. They're cautious, damn them, and they've caused more than a few deaths, of that I'm convinced.

It's thanks to this certainty that my fingernails are long and tough; I keep them like this because I must also be cautious, for any cook could become transformed overnight into the steeliest of enemies. Death by betrayal is but a wink away, and therefore I must be wary and take advantage of this confinement to sharpen my nails like the very knives used in the kitchens of the senior cooks. Because there are ranks among the cooks—apprentices and favorites—and the apprentices may not use knives freely; knives can only be wielded by senior cooks. They sharpen and brandish and use them as though manipulating life and the end of life. This is true, of course, which is why they keep the knives hidden tenderly and lovingly under their armpits, held in place by a thin strap; they love them like naked girls, because apart from the knives there are no other offensive metals in the house. All of us eat with our fingers, and kill each other with the strength of our hands, something which would be extremely difficult for me, because I am weak, I'm just a wandering gaze, which is to say I'm nothing but a walking misery. You heard it, it's what she said, I'm just a gaze that wanders. She shouted this with a conciliatory laugh as I fled from the clothed ones.

But they're such cretins and yet so dangerous, these brutish cooks, attentive servants to the clothed ones; they spend their whole lives striving to please with an invented dish, and they boast about their recipes, presenting them once elaborated before their diners with long-winded dedications. They argue among themselves to the point of tears, to the point of rage and cruel threats—which never amount to anything—over the paternity of this or that dish, and they spend hours pondering in front of the stoves, because their imaginations are nothing but a larder dedicated exclusively to the fine palates of the visitors. They say that one of the most respected cooks—known as Saurio by the clothed ones—is in the habit of using children's buttocks in one of his most esteemed dishes; but none of the visitors knows this, and it would be very difficult to discover where in the recipe the buttocks are called for (surely Saurio mashes and dissolves them in cows' tongues or duck liver, or bulls' testicles, or who knows, who can know this—many in this house spend their time in idle gossip).

It's only natural that the visitors react warmly to the culinary genius of the cooks: they reward them, seating them at their tables and embracing them as if they were equals, incentivizing them by claiming that only cooks can become immortal among men, and as a consequence they continue to possess excellent informants inside our house, loyal concealers of kitchen utensils—always so susceptible to being transformed into weapons of war. And yet, there is no need for the clothed ones to harbor such fears; no naked one, to my knowledge, would ever think of converting a kitchen knife into a knife of war. If that were the case, we in this house would soon witness the disappearance of all the knives, forks, and spoons used by the clothed ones at the table, as well as the scissors, frying pans, and fireplace pokers. The clothed ones are cautious and deceitful; they've persuaded our very cooks to despise us, as if they were just another bunch of clothed ones, voluntarily naked in order to control us.

TODAY, IT SEEMS, I SHOULD FEEL MORE HATRED TOWARD the naked ones in this house than the clothed ones who torture them. If one of the most powerful reasons for my confinement is my fear and absolute certainty of one day being selected to go outside, another must be the profound uneasiness provoked in me by the sight of naked ones wandering like nomads inside their own house. The agglomeration of armpits. The sweat. The faces that ask for nothing—except to eat—and show nothing—except their desire to eat. The intemperate tangling of bodies with two sexes that succumb to the final caress and then part ways as strangers. The impertinent animal smile. The quarrels. The bawling of idiots. The laments of the sick. The noisy death of an old-timer. The victorious yawns of the cooks when they've finished their work. The harsh, stinking sounds of those sitting grub-like in the latrines. The adolescents, who have yet to decide whether to be more man than woman, or the reverse, combing their hair sadly in front of the mirror.

The old women scrutinizing the fringes of both their sexes, in search of more lice to eat. The drool of stupidity on the lips of a beautiful girl, who makes love to herself using her virile part, indulging it and caressing it eternally, before hemorrhaging from love, and dying. Another girl pees while standing, through both her sexes, from the rafters, over everybody's heads. Another girl squats to pee. Another scratches herself there, before the boisterous expectation of some masturbating youths. A belch. A sigh. A wallop. Beneath each old-timer there's a great resounding fart. A woman suckling her babe is assaulted from behind. A small child is too. A birth, a new howl inside the house. An unclaimed cackle. A months-old child observes the flame of a torch for the first time. Newborns proliferate. There are toddlers who can already walk, yet their compassionate mothers still carry them on their backs and shoulders to keep them from being trampled to death. And there's the fear, finally, the purest, most elemental, grotesque fear of the pain of approaching torture, of the lack of bread, of that fatal hour when someone points to you and says: "You have to go out."

And, in spite of everything, when it is me who comes out of the wardrobe because someone has left the house to run the errands, I generally head to the front door and try to follow every step and hesitation of the naked one with my gaze; I watch through the cracks in the door, which allow me to survey most of the street. I follow the naked one's footsteps until he disappears from view; from that moment on I imagine the naked one's progress and, without understanding exactly why, I feel pity. I feel, in spite of everything, a great sense of shame and indignation for us all; I imagine that the naked one is me, and I convince myself of it to the point of convulsion. My imagination is my most potent enemy, for it often places me in the skin of the naked one who is outside, and I suffer as much—or more—than he does. I am he, and I slip furtively along the streets, more alone than ever, under cold as heavy as stone, making my way quickly through the icy looks of the clothed ones, imploring with every gesture of my eyes and hands that they allow me to continue, that they allow me to reach the shop and the shopkeeper charged with supplying our house, or that they at least decide quickly and torture me without killing me, or that my face and figure bore them so they allow me to return, conveniently stocked up, or that they find themselves busy with tasks far more important to them, a wedding, for example, the celebration of a birth, or a death, above all, for just as our naked deaths go unnoticed, with stealthily nocturnal burials, the deaths of the clothed ones are suffered with shrieks of sorrow, processions, fainting, sometimes with speeches meant to uphold the memory of the departed, repeating that no, no they aren't dead, that they live and will go on living forever in everybody's memory, eternally.

And only when the naked one in question returns to the house do I go back to my wardrobe and breathe easy, perhaps unsettled by a morbid curiosity to learn the final details of what happened to him out there. And my eagerness to find out never goes unsatisfied, for it so happens I'm lucky enough to occupy a wardrobe beside one of the largest kitchens, where there is constant warmth, a favorite place for the naked ones who return alive—with boxes of supplies inexplicably at their sides—to recount their adventures. I know this kitchen is the best-stocked, and that no surreptitious deaths have taken place within its precincts. I also know of other corners with other pieces of furniture like the one I inhabit, or nooks formed in the walls, lodgings—in any case—which have been conveniently prepared so other naked ones can be kept apart when we have visitors. My wardrobe isn't the only hiding place. They need more attics, alcoves, and screens; all sorts of cages and apertures are created for the express purpose of storing naked ones when there is a party so the clothed ones can enter and move freely about the house, breathe and make themselves comfortable, look us over and select us at their leisure. In the very rafters, at their dusty, grimy bases, many young naked ones must find a space, generally squatting, their necks craning downward, their faces intent on not missing a single detail. Some hang tethered by their arms and ankles. Others improvise a sort of pallet, and remain like that, face down, throughout the proceedings. They're like a separate village inside the house, a curious species of animal, an extraordinary colony of bats—large and pale— their eyes shining in the steam from pots bubbling noisily beneath their bodies, from the smoke of cigars, the vapors from the breath of other bodies that tangle and untangle, cry out, go silent, throbbing and living and surviving beneath transitory deaths. My companions in the wardrobe (when there is a party) are never the same; only very occasionally does one of them accidentally return. I can usually recognize them by the profile of their noses, by their odors, by the feel of their bodies, the tone of their voices, the resonance of their yawns, their laughter, their whimpering, because that's all they are: individual laughs and whimpers. But only I inhabit this wardrobe voluntarily. The rest wait patiently for the opportunity at the next party not to be hidden, and therefore to be able to partake in such events as a dance, a chat, an argument, a joke, a newly invented caress, a misunderstanding, a clothed one's displeasure, and, above all, a torture inside the house. Those selected to be hidden are the biggest slackers that week, those who let their guard down at the crucial moment. They're surprised, and abruptly shoved into the nearest "naked storing" niche, or hoisted by dozens of hands up onto one of the ceiling beams, or submerged in any piece of furniture in the house; they're transported, finally, like retreating flags, a multitude of hands delivering them, receiving them, before they're deposited (as in a game) in whichever corner they happen to land. They resign themselves, they don't protest, although sometimes they let out a nostalgic whimper, an expression of their disappointment at the discomfort they'll have to put up with during the night. It's true that none of the hidden ever suffer the misfortune of falling into disgrace, or of being tortured or subjected to public derision (many old-timers and women hide for just this reason, to feel protected), but the majority swear out loud never again to be distracted or captured by anyone; they consider it a catastrophe to find themselves far from the tumult, from their destiny, perhaps from the extra plates of food, and so they repeat their oath never again to allow unexpected hands to capture them and tear them away from the game.

I don't need to be caught. With me, these lengths aren't necessary: everyone in the house knows I'm always willing to go back into the wardrobe, if I happen to be outside, which is rare.

I only leave through my window.

This window is me, taking steps.

THERE IS, HOWEVER, A REMOTE FURY THAT COMPELS ME to leave the wardrobe and offend the clothed ones during their parties, even if it means exposing myself. Once, I opened the door abruptly, intentionally, banging an adrift dancing woman in the nose. My frightened companions crouched together more tightly; the clothed one let out a howl of rage and pain, but didn't call for help. She was drunk, searching vociferously for Jesús. Defiant and lewd, she spat on me, said "Monster," and closed the door in my face.

During the most recent night of partying, we opened the door, woken by desperate voices. "Someone's being tortured," one of us said. Through the throng of bodies swirling around the antagonists, it was difficult to get any more details; the shouting, the naked ones' fear and vehement desire to distance themselves prevented us from hearing clearly. It surprised us to discover that these antagonists were a clothed and a naked one; the naked one said nothing, what could he say, and the clothed one was reproaching him. A number of his companions interjected, approving or disapproving of his ideas. He was proposing all sorts of torture, threatening the naked one with instant death. He was beside himself. An important man of law, and one of the most frequent visitors to the house, his name was Teodosio Monteverde. I slipped out of the wardrobe and was able to watch as I pleased: at the feet of the persecuted naked one lay the body of the Dwarf—apparently lifeless—inside a circle of light produced by the flickering torches. I immediately realized the dispute must relate to this silent dwarf. I remembered her from before. She was blonde and slender; it was easy to mistake her for a child, especially if you saw her from behind, for on her face the expression of a lascivious woman glowed like a caress. Whenever he came to our house, Teodosio Monteverde would spend the entire evening with the Dwarf sitting on his knee, both in silence, contemplating each other intently, as if they were conversing in some archaic manner. Occasionally Monteverde would run his fingers through her hair, or allow her to stroke his beard, scratch behind his ears, or swing from his neck. Sometimes they would remain hidden beneath a table, nobody seeing them again until morning, when the visitor abandoned their hiding place and left the house, always in silence, without even saying goodbye. You could almost be certain they'd never exchanged two words; they merely observed each other with intense concentration, perhaps each stupefied by the other.

Now, in his desperation Monteverde wasn't just raging

against the world. He was drunk, his lips wet with saliva; his fat, hairy hands twitched, tore at his beard that was long and stiff as a brush, and then hung in the air, like wings, before pointing to the naked one standing in front of him, terrified, with the Dwarf lying still between them. But when Monteverde advanced resolutely upon the naked one, the Dwarf, who had appeared dead, let out a cry, threw herself at his feet, and began pleading for the naked one's life. This seemed to disconcert Monteverde, who took three steps backwards, with difficulty, for the Dwarf was still tangled around his legs; but he composed himself and, in a trembling voice, ordered the cook, Saurio, to hand over his knife immediately. Saurio, ever diligent, gave him the knife, while Monteverde ferociously disentangled himself from the Dwarf and pounced on the naked one, running him through. The naked one was as tall as Monteverde, although less sinewy, and much younger. He didn't make a single sound, just managing to embrace Monteverde tightly, as the blade of the knife pierced his flesh beneath his left nipple, right to the heart. They remained locked in an embrace, moving backwards and forwards, like a pair of clumsy wooden puppets. During this absurd dance, the dying naked one's eyes never left the kneeling Dwarf, who was bathed in tears, surrounded by a light that appeared to redden unexpectedly. The pathetic dance between the drunken Monteverde and the naked one, now dead, continued for another minute, absurdly, while a number of the clothed ones shook their heads disapprovingly, or applauded. The milling naked ones began to calm down, and it seemed everything would go on as before, in spite of the death, in spite of this crazy dance that Monteverde's inebriation made all the more zigzagging and real.

I managed to overhear that Teodosio Monteverde had arrived late. That he wasn't even expected. That all of a sudden they'd seen him arrive, drunk, and shouting for the Dwarf. That he undressed in a flash, leaving on nothing but his tie, and began to search frantically for her, throwing all the groups into disarray, shoving his way through, interrupting every conversation, accosting clothed and naked alike. Some of his friends surrounded him, assisting him in his search. It was impossible for the Dwarf to be hiding in a niche, a piece of furniture, or up in the rafters, for she was a *favorita*, and this protected her from being hidden away by force. So it was extraordinary that she didn't appear, small as she might be. Ten-year-old girls suffered the worst effects of Monteverde's anxiety. In fact, he confused the first one he spotted with the Dwarf: the little girl was trying to play on her own, with a wooden hoop, her back turned, and, with a roar of delight, the visitor in the red tie hoisted her precariously into the air and was about to cover her with kisses, burble sweet nothings in her ear, when he realized his mistake and, letting out an anguished snort, hurled the girl up over everybody's heads, and then kept throwing more girls left and right. And to this day nobody knows what happened to those girls, if they were fortunate in their respective falls, or if someone considerate devoted himself to catching them as they came hurtling down, frazzled and terrified; or if, on the contrary, everyone was left paralyzed by the clothed one's wrath, and stood watching mutely as an increasing number of girls came down from the air, crashing against the walls like bundles of sobs.

The visitor ended up finding his *favorita* in one of the darkest galleries, in the very corner they themselves frequented. He surprised her writhing in pleasure, crouched on top of a reclining naked one, not even a clothed one, which would have been tolerable, but just some naked one (raising the possibility that there is also love between naked ones). A miserable naked one, then, was who had appropriated the Dwarf, the pair of them bubbling with happiness, as if in ecstasy. Their four interwoven sexes flooded Teodosio Monteverde with hatred. And so began the tragedy that finished with that danse macabre, under the light of the torches, before the imploring gaze of the Dwarf. What happened next may seem inconceivable, though the clothed ones who were present can attest to it all, as can the naked ones who only exist today because they survived the massacre: in one of those rare luminous flashes of reason that appear in the midst of inebriation, the visitor must have caught sight of himself, as if from afar, enacting that dance with a dead man—that firm and perfect embrace that had already gone on too long—and then tried desperately to escape from the arms of the corpse, without managing to do so in his first attempt, becoming almost terrified, progressively disgusted by the body and the warm blood that gripped him with the remote strength of a last desire. And it was impossible—or so it appeared—to break free, for he tried three more times, without success. And it was the Dwarf, above all, who seemed most surprised by the dance; it even appeared she was hoping the explanation for that persistent embrace was none other than the naked one's being alive, that her naked one was still living and forcing Monteverde to dance grotesquely before her. But she soon lost that hope, for Monteverde finally managed to free himself, and was now attempting to throw the naked one into one of the ovens in the kitchen. Again, the rest of the naked ones retreated in shock; Monteverde's companions furrowed their brows, disapproving of the incineration, because none of them wanted to sample a dinner cooked over the embers of a naked one instead of charcoal, as it's supposed to be. However, Teodosio Monteverde was far too drunk to stuff the corpse into the oven. He teetered precariously, and it almost seemed that he too would end up in the fire; but he regained his balance at the last moment, took two steps back, and then lost all control of himself, for he began to spin with the naked one on his back, propelled by inertia, blindly, creating in their twirling a single body with four bladelike arms and two heads resting against each other, oscillating . The four tangled, bumbling legs created a kind of opening through the rest of the bodies that could no longer retreat any further and were attempting to rid themselves of the pair, dispatching them from place to place, in a circle of desperation, for they all strove not to be left next to Monteverde's furious face and the other bloody face of the naked one. Yet no matter how hard he struggled to stop himself, Monteverde was unable to do anything but accelerate his circular journey, and so it was that he ended up in the area where we found ourselves, and only there did he collapse, along with his naked one, both absolutely submerged in this precipice of bodies that is me.

What happened after that, nobody knows except me. If you were to ask any naked ones who survived the catastrophe, they would only say they saw the visitor emerge from among all the bodies, headless, brandishing a bloody knife, and then he was gone. Monteverde's eyes, ears, lips, and tongue were in our power, but no one will ever find that head. His friends will never be able to recover it; unknown naked ones, shrouded in the momentary disorder, made short work of it as a snack. Not even in his wildest dreams could Teodosio Monteverde have imagined his head would end up separated from his body and then in the guts of various nameless naked ones. And it was I who instigated them: I said "*Devour*," after using my nails on Monteverde's fleshy neck. Only the headless body, the knife, and the red tie were recovered. A contingent of clothed ones arrived, armed to the teeth, charged with ensuring the nocturnal peace. It wasn't the first time they'd burst into the house at the slightest indication of disorder. I watched as several naked ones fell, without a whimper, their heads masterfully severed by the sharp steel of the clothed ones. There was a terrified tumult, and this allowed the clothed ones to continue their beheading work with greater tranquility. The majority were surprised from behind; as for the naked ones attacked head on, they never did a thing to defend themselves. The quiet deaths piled up. Nobody fled. Where to? The house was our last and only refuge.

The clothed ones eventually grew tired of the beheadings; the killing of hundreds of naked ones was far from a persuasive act; it was even possible to consider it a waste of naked ones, for their deaths should only be conceived for the pleasure and distraction afforded by torture, for the very refinement of the apparatus and methods of torture. On the other hand, Teodosio Monteverde's death—his mysterious decapitation—more than justified such an outcome, such genocide; never before had a clothed one died at the hands of naked ones. Which of the naked ones was responsible? There isn't much strength in my hands, but hatred is another strength, perhaps even more powerful, for its origins are in the deepest reaches of our blood.

Since that last party, the cooks have assumed responsibility for burying the decapitated bodies in the shortest time possible, but not their heads, for these are to remain forever scattered across the floors, as an example. An example? Only time will tell whether we would ever dare to eat them.

None of the most coveted naked ones were killed, those who regularly take part in the beauty pageants the clothed ones organize in order to feast their eyes. They're all still here, walking together in a group: Aguamarina, the Bird, Nebulosa, the Panther, Nutria, Sea Cow, Ibis, Palm Tree, Oasis, Sandia, Poppy, Belladonna, Fennel, Salvia, Melon, Water Lily, Chrysanthemum, Honeysuckle, the Comet, Iris, Cinder, Meridiana, Pearl, Dominga, Hilaria, Boa, Silencia, and Iluminada, women who, owing to the sibylline tenderness of their work, have earned their names among the clothed ones, along with men such as Adonis, Pelagius, Pigtail, Cajetan, Flax, Cedar, Orange Grove, Ben, Centurion, Lucius, Murray, Coyote, Basalt, Felix, Jade, Cricket, Dodo, the Goose, Loggerhead, Raccoon, the Mute, Justus, and Maximilian, all of whom earned their names for their exquisite cowardice, for being more man or woman, depending on the whims and demands of the visitors. Old Jesús is still alive, sitting and eating, as are Saurio and the cooks. As for the rest of us survivors, all that surrounds us is hunger, a pitiless hunger that has already begun to bear its white teeth in the faces of the youngest, who are immersed in a frightening greed. The heads of the decapitated naked ones greet the new day perfectly peeled, like enormous peach stones from which all the juice and flesh have been extracted, and which are licked over and over again in search of the memory of that juice and that flesh.

A new watchfulness nests inside the cooks; they know perfectly well, as does everyone else living here, that Teodosio Monteverde's death occurred at the hands of a naked one, and if this naked one felt no qualms about taking the life of a clothed one (a man of law no less), he'd have no problem taking the life of some favorite, or *favorita*, or even a cook, why not?

BUT NOW THE NAKED ONES OF THIS HOUSE ARE STARING at me. At this very moment they're forming a ring around me; they raise their eyes to the open door of my wardrobe.

"You're going out," says one of the cooks. "You're going out tomorrow."

At this there's a ripple of happiness, the peculiar happiness of the naked ones in this house when they haven't been selected to go outside. I see a vision approaching from one of the corners of the kitchen, transfigured by a smile that strikes me as fierce, for being unknown: perhaps it's a loving smile. She is the reason I've been chosen. She's wearing the same veil she wore the night she prevented them from coming after me; her voice is the one I remember, sultry, and her eyes—the only living things in her veiled face— are the same, as beautiful as they are merciless. Finally she removes the veil. A pale, oval face appears, and behind it a head of thick, curly hair, with ringlets like fronds of a golden fern. She has a long neck, a pensive brow; the long lashes above her green eyes tremble. She raises her eyes and flashes them like flames on my eyes, on the whole of my face, which stands out because of my stature among the eager sea of other eyes and heads. Her lips split suddenly like a fruit down the middle; I think she might be about to sing; nothing can be heard, nobody hears a thing, but it's safe to say that everyone is sure of hearing something, a kind of victorious song, which is also an irrefutable accusation, for it carries no words.

"You're scared," she says afterwards.

"Why."

"Because tomorrow you'll have to go outside."

"It's true. I'm scared."

There's a pitiless silence, and then I ask:

"Why do you want to know?"

"Because I'm scared for you, too."

"Who are you?" I ask. And her voice:

"I don't know. I would've liked to have spoken to you in another time, to discover who I am."

When she left the house, the pupils of her eyes regarded me far more attentively. This was because they were no longer anywhere but inside my mind, forever, like a life sentence. Her eyes bade me a flaming farewell, as did her hands, flying over this whole inscrutable chasm that is memory, burying me within an inescapable dream. Because minutes before she left, she had led me to a secluded corner and for the first time became naked in front of me; she revealed herself without any veil or piece of clothing that could distinguish her as a clothed one, she opened, she parted before me like water. A sour sleepy smell of crushed grass came from her body, like the last light from a candle when it goes out. Her warmth was the first thing, then her skin. Her hand, as stealthy as a wing, made its way inside my body.

I never knew which of my two sexes had really moved her.

Crouching, like some unknown animal, her happiness was complete, and yet, she wasn't smiling.

"Don't you find me beautiful?" she asked.

"I don't know," I said.

"Do you find men more beautiful?"

"I can't tell you that either," I replied again. And she shrugged.

"When you find out tell me," she then pleaded, almost in distress. "I think to myself: I simply can't believe he's not in love with me. Or should I say she? I've felt your love from the first moment you heard my voice. Haven't you ever been in love?"

"No," I said. "Not with any man or woman."

"Who else could you be in love with?" she yelled at me.

"Myself," I answered, and she raised a hand to her mouth in horror. Then she revealed a smile of commiseration, as if she were making fun of herself.

"You are the greatest exception," she said, as if describing a tragedy. "Only this house could have produced you. You're the most extraordinary peal of laughter reverberating on earth today. We've been tracking you for a long time, but now my kind no longer wishes to allow you to talk, or breathe. You're dangerous, beloved monster, and I always dreamed of you. My sophistry was futile. I told them that of all the naked ones you were the marvelous exception; that your profound rebellion was a matter for study. I fought for you, believe me."

She folded her hands and bit her lips until they bled, in a gesture of anticipated defeat.

"Tomorrow you must go outside," she said. "And I can no longer save you."

Without waiting for me to reply, she left.

I stood before the great mirror of the house, surrounded by naked ones on all sides, I stood before the great mirror and contemplated myself for the first time, astonished, and I laughed. I ran toward my own image and then I kissed myself. My lips kissed my image on the cold mirror, and I experienced all of love, without any fear of losing that love, for I myself, with myself, was that love. For I do not wish to—nor can I ever—separate myself, not even through death. I am always indissoluble, she and he, me.

I WONDER HOW MUCH TIME HAS PASSED. IT'S NOT POSSI-
ble to guess the time by the light; light here is perishable, it
comes from a distant torch that, sooner or later, will go out.
I cannot imagine how the clothed ones will finish me off.
My fears rise like water in a well, and I'm right down at the
bottom, tied up. I'll be taken prisoner. As I step out into the
morning all the windows will open and the heads of prat-
tling women will emerge like wet birds, and a multitude of
children, or a river of cries, will run behind me. All the doors
of all the houses will open; more and more clothed ones will
appear, perplexed or curious, the majority of them furious.
Young women, their youth pert in their breasts, all wearing
black hats and veils, will clamor to recommend an original
method of torture. A great murmur will incline all the faces,
as if a great wind were leveling a field of wheat. The eldest
will brandish their canes, vermin ready to take the intemperate leap; they'll observe me with drooling attention. "It's

true," they'll say, "you have the same two sexes and the hatred possessed by the first inhabitant of your house, the one who engendered you and your kind. You're courting rebellion. Of all the naked ones, you are therefore the most undesirable and the most dangerous." And they'll have to get rid of me as quickly as possible, for as long as I'm breathing they will never be free to breathe with impunity. The most despotic and resentful of their housemaids will offend me. Their priests caution that it's highly likely the earth will tremble when I die, or perhaps it will suddenly become dark, and a great orange light will burst from my chest tearing down the churches and desecrating their sacred objects. My naked image will be a burning recollection that will torment their hearts while they sleep, which is to say forever. And then, when my body has been buried far from its head, like a perpetual division of the sexes, once my blood has dried, no danger will remain, and from the land there shall be no more response than a memory. Then the crowd will disperse.

I look at my fingers. I am alone for the last time in the wardrobe. I peer through my window; I'm surrounded by the resplendence of shining torches; some voices can be heard; it's not yet dawn. This memory must be publicly ridiculed. They'll hang it by its feet for days, beneath the pestilent onslaught of vultures. I'll become an invisible naked one, a breath of air. I know they've begun to speak of me in the past tense.

A mischievous, thousand-year-old voice impels me to scream in dialogue with myself; a voice that is not me, but is me, that makes fun of me, and of the other voice, of all those that are me. I myself console myself, caress and sympathize with myself. I'm a devoted delirium, a monstrous idyll. I reunite and reconcile. Whenever I experience this attraction, there follows a useless and tortuous battle in which the love I feel only for myself, my indecipherable union, finally triumphs. And it is now, alone with myself, that I resolve that love. I'm aware of pairs of pupils floating nearby. Inside this wardrobe I walk along burning streets, whose surfaces are covered in coffins, and many of the coffins are rotten, so sometimes I fall, with a scream, because it's a shock to discover that the coffins are inhabited, not by corpses, but by beings identical to myself, terrified by the way they are awakened; some even let out screams of horror on realizing an identical being has fallen on them, and their screams merge with mine—as I fall—so that there is a double scream, a double horror.

The dawn is mournful, like me. I've wound up unable to distinguish which of my voices is the one that speaks. At this moment, at least, I don't know. And the voices are mocking. But mocking whom? They're mocking me, which is to say us. The cooks open the wardrobe door and force me out. There's an instruction: I must kneel. One of them, Saurio, wishes to offend me. As the other naked ones clear the way, he says:

"We shall eat four hundred and twenty-six tons of pork in your honor."

I'm already kneeling and I place my head between my hands.

"They're going to drive you mad," says Jesús, from his spot near the kitchen.

The air is full of voices. My reason indicates one path. Other thoughts show me another path. I know I should forget myself in order to survive. Other naked bodies point the direction I should follow. At the end, there is only the abyss. Something, or someone, from within the spongy violet fog, is pulling the strings from which my steps hang. The oldest of our women yell at me, toothless. I don't understand them. With their torches they trace strange symbols in the air. Eternal fugitive, vague memory. Nobody comes to say goodbye. I rail against the naked ones. I lash out, and they retaliate. It's like trying to tear apart a labyrinth woven from identical beings, my very likenesses. But they continue to push me toward the door. To them I'm nothing but a perishing memory. Where does the fabulous, throbbing trap that awaits me lie? My hands tremble, open on the lintel. I'm still kneeling.

Now a multitude of clothed ones contemplates me.

I stand up, place my nails against my neck, where the blood flows: I'm still alive; my blood should scream something. I should tear out an eye and throw it to the crowd. My gesture causes chaos in the audience. I live. I am alive in the midst of their wars.

When I place my nails against my neck I hear their anguish through the purple fog. My hands are my masters, not them. One morning my bloody scalp will wave like a pennant in the hands of some exalted maiden; but today, my formidable foes, today it will pain you to the point of asphyxiation that I condemn and execute myself of my own free will.

They rush to surround me. The skies of the world come down like pieces of a shattered mirror, my nails bury me, my sexes are united. There's a death rattle, and a profound, long-lasting sadness comes over their faces, and this itself induces a kind of comic mask. There are so many sighs, so many mouths immersed in laments, it's as though all of the faces were laughing at once. My death is a calamity: everywhere, unrestrained women shriek, as do children, as do the old. It's as though nobody can breathe, because I die publicly, because I love myself as I do so, stubborn as a stone. Skinny dogs sniff at me. In my ears there's a coitus of whining insects; on my lips, cockroaches implant their hieroglyphs like invisible words; crows balance scathingly on branches, cats chase each other passionately, and buzzards draw rings of feathers around my bifurcated corpse. If I could retrace my steps, I would discover I was never born, that I've been here since before forever, that I was the first of the first of the first, and also the last. So I shall be ready to laugh victoriously at the world, but my death will remind me that as well as eternal, I am also dead, and will suffer for an instant the tranquility of finding myself dying. For no sooner will I speak—as just another inhabitant of the realm of death—than the voices of the dead will be heard in unison like a soft murmur of greeting and the uproar will be symphonic and explicit and I will understand that I've been resuscitated into another life, not corporeal, but rather sonorous.

I die and night and silence fall, with no window; now the voices of the dead are quiet. Now the enormous black world that surrounds me is the same black wardrobe I formerly occupied. I finally recognize the profound difference between the beings that live and breathe in unison with me. I am alone, with them. I desperately integrate into myself, not realizing that in doing so I myself disintegrate; I unite with myself upon dying, because no other memory exists to intervene, because something like a river leads me toward myself, because I am an abyss and allow myself to be carried by the current of my attractions, my upward cataclysm, following the subterranean vortex of my voices that pours into myself. Terrified with love as I die, I follow each and every one of the channels I present to myself, spilling into myself, slipping wet and boiling, depositing myself for all eternity within my-basin-my-bed-my-grave, losing myself in me like an underwater scream, transported like a thunderstorm, dispersed, struck, dead. Dead, above all, because at the same time as I invade myself, I feel that I am invaded mortally by life, my compact flame of light that wounds me and takes control of my beings and hurls them one-and-two into the infinite converted into two screams, each the delicate assassin of the other, for the universe is he and is she and is incandescent and can be deciphered like the final tomb, because I feel that I die and resuscitate and as I die definitively I myself inscribe in blood—in the street, before the world—the happy epitaph: here lie the most furtive of lovers, the last of the last.

CHÍA, 1988–1990